Mr. Klutz Is Nuts!

Mr. Klutz Is Nuts!

Dan Gutman

Pictures by
Jim Paillot

SCHOLASTIC INC.

New York   Toronto   London   Auckland   Sydney
Mexico City   New Delhi   Hong Kong   Buenos Aires

ISBN 0-439-70043-4

Text copyright © 2004 by Dan Gutman.
Illustrations copyright © 2004 by Jim Paillot.
All rights reserved. Published by Scholastic Inc.,
557 Broadway, New York, NY 10012, by arrangement with
HarperCollins Publishers. SCHOLASTIC and associated logos
are trademarks and/or registered trademarks of Scholastic Inc.

24 23 22 21 20 19 18 17   11 12 13 14 15 16/0

Printed in the U.S.A.   40

First Scholastic printing, November 2004

Typography by Nicole de las Heras

To Emma

Contents

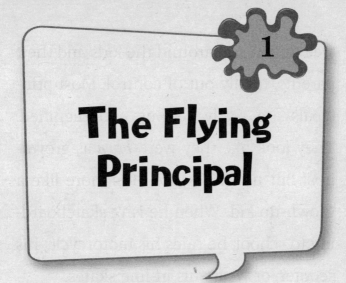

The Flying Principal

"Watch out!" somebody screamed.

Mr. Klutz, the principal of my school, was tearing down the sidewalk on a skateboard! It was early morning, just before the school bell was about to ring.

Mr. Klutz must have built up too much speed coming down the hill. He was weaving in and around the kids and their parents, totally out of control. Most principals are really serious and dignified. They look like they were *born* as grown-ups! But not Mr. Klutz. He's more like a grown-up kid. When he isn't skateboarding to school, he rides his motorcycle, his scooter, or wears his in-line skates.

"Runaway principal!" some kid shouted. "Run for your lives!"

The skateboard must have hit a crack in the sidewalk, because the next thing anybody knew, Mr. Klutz was flying through the air like a superhero. Kids and their parents were diving out of his way. Dogs were running in all directions.

Mr. Klutz crash-landed in the bushes at the front of the school. Luckily he was wearing a helmet, and he had knee pads and elbow pads on over his clothes. Everybody stopped for a second, because Mr. Klutz was just lying there in the

bushes without moving. We weren't sure if he was alive.

"Good morning, Mr. Klutz," said Mrs. Cooney, the school nurse, as she walked past.

"Good morning, Mrs. Cooney," he replied.

"Beautiful day, isn't it?"

"Lovely."

Then Mr. Klutz got up, brushed himself off, and walked up the front steps, like it was totally normal for a principal to skateboard to school and crash headfirst into the bushes.

Mr. Klutz is nuts!

Big Trouble

"That's the last straw, A.J.," my teacher, Miss Daisy, told me. "I want you to go to the principal's office!"

"I didn't do anything!" I protested.

My name is A.J. and I hate school. Why do we have to learn so much stuff? If you ask me, by the time you get to second grade you already know enough stuff to last you a lifetime. School is way overrated.

My mom says that all eight-year-old boys have to go to school, so I guess there's nothing I can do about it. But when I grow up, I'm going to be a professional hockey player. You don't have to

know how to read or write or do math to shoot a puck into a net.

Actually, that's what I was doing when my teacher, Miss Daisy, sent me to the principal's office.

You see, me and my friends Michael and Ryan were playing hockey with a tennis ball during recess. We were shooting the ball at a tree to score a goal. I shot one wild, and it landed over by a bunch of girls in our class.

"Ouch! That hit me!" shouted this girl named Annette. She was rubbing her leg like she had been hit by a train or something. It was just a tennis ball! Annette is such a crybaby.

"Hey, A.J.!" Michael hollered. "That counts as a goal!"

"How come?" I asked. "I missed the tree."

"Well, you did hit the puck into Annette. Get it? Annette? A net? Annette?" Well, after me and Ryan got it, we thought that was just about the funniest joke in the history of the world.

Miss Daisy didn't think it was very funny, though. She was already mad at me because I had forgotten to bring in a current-event article for the third week in a row.

That's when she said it was the last straw and I had to go to Mr. Klutz's office.

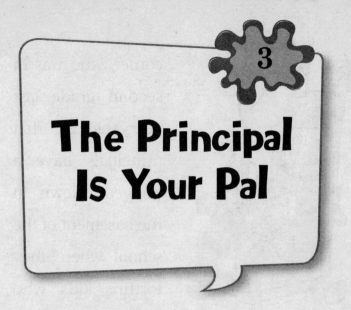

The Principal Is Your Pal

The principal is like the king of the school. He gets to tell everybody what to do and where to go. That is cool! If I can't be a professional hockey player when I grow up, I want to be a principal so I can boss teachers around.

My friend Billy from around the

corner, who was in second grade last year, told me that principals have a dungeon down in the basement of the school where they torture kids who misbehave. I don't know if Billy's telling the truth or not. But one time we had gym class and we passed by this open door in the basement and there were all kinds of scary-looking things in there. Michael said he saw chains hanging from the ceiling over a chair with straps on the arms and legs, so I guess that's what Mr. Klutz uses to torture bad kids.

I was scared. I had never been to the principal's office before. On the way there, I stopped into the boy's bathroom. Maybe I could dig a tunnel out of the school and escape, I thought. My friend Billy told me he saw that in a war movie once. These guys dug their way out of prison camp with a spoon. But I didn't have a spoon. And I didn't want to touch the floor of the bathroom anyway. Yuck!

When I got to Mr. Klutz's office, his secretary made me sit in a chair for about a million hours. Mr. Klutz's door was closed the whole time. I wondered if he was torturing some other kid. I didn't hear any screams or anything.

Finally the secretary said I could go inside. I opened the door and was surprised to see Mr. Klutz was hanging upside down from a bar near the ceiling. He had on boots that were attached to the bar.

"What are you doing up there?" I asked.

"Oh, just hanging around," Mr. Klutz said as he pulled himself out of his boots and jumped down onto the floor. "When the blood rushes to my head, it helps me think."

Well, I know that blood rushing to your head doesn't help you grow hair, because Mr. Klutz had no hair on his

head at all. He was bald as a balloon. Mr. Klutz's office looked pretty much like my dad's office, except he had a big snowboarding poster on the wall and a foosball table in the corner. Oh, and he also had a punching bag with a face on it.

Come to think of it, it didn't look anything like my dad's office.

I kept my head down when he told me to take a seat, so he would feel sorry for me. When you get into trouble, always keep your head down, because if grown-ups feel sorry for you they won't punish you as badly.

"Miss Daisy told me why you're here," Mr. Klutz said, "but I'd like to hear your side of the story."

"Miss Daisy thinks I stole some straws," I told him.

"What makes you think that, A.J.?"

"Well, she was all mad at me and she said, 'That's the last straw!' Then she told me to go to your office. I swear I didn't take any straws. I don't even know where she keeps the straws."

"I see," Mr. Klutz said, rubbing his chin. "I thought it had something to do with a hockey game that got out of control. And there's this little matter of forgetting to bring in current events."

"Well, that too."

Mr. Klutz didn't look like he was going to torture me. In fact, he didn't look mad at all.

"You may not believe this," he told me, "but I was a boy once."

"Just once?" I asked. "I'm a boy *all* the time."

"No, what I mean is, I used to be young like you."

"I'll bet you were really good in school," I said.

"No, actually, it was just the opposite," the principal told me. "I didn't like school at all, and I wasn't a very good student."

"Really?" I figured that anybody who grew up to be a principal must have loved school as a kid. Why else would you want to hang around a school all day as a grown-up? Except maybe to boss teachers around.

"When I was a boy, I could never sit

still," Mr. Klutz said. "I wanted to run around all the time. I didn't have the motivation to do my schoolwork. Do you know what motivation is, A.J.?"

"It's like a motor inside you that makes you want to do stuff," I said. "That's why it's called motor-vation."

"I guess you could say that," Mr. Klutz said. "Sometimes my mother would give me a little reward if I did a good job on my homework. A piece of candy, for instance. You see, while I didn't like school, I certainly did like candy. So I would try hard in school in order to get the candy. Does that make sense to you?"

"Well, sure."

"A.J., if I were to give you some candy, do you think it might help you remember to bring in your current event next time?"

"My parents told me never to take candy from strangers," I told him.

"I'm not a stranger," Mr. Klutz said. "Did you ever hear anyone say 'your principal is your pal'? If you need to spell the word *principal*, you can always remember, your princi*pal* is your *p-a-l*. Get it?"

"Well, if you put it that way, I suppose I could take some candy."

Mr. Klutz reached into his desk drawer and pulled out a chocolate bar. It was the kind with marshmallow inside, and caramel. My mouth was watering. "Go easy with the hockey. And let's see if you can remember to bring in that current event tomorrow," he said as he handed me the candy bar. "Don't tell anyone about this, okay? It's

just a little secret between you and me."

"Okay!"

I ran out of the office just in case he had only given me the candy bar so he could tie me to a chair and torture me.

The Present

When I got back to the class, everybody looked at me. I guess they wanted to see if I was crying or bleeding or anything.

"Did Klutz bring you down into his torture chamber?" Ryan whispered when I sat in my seat.

"Nope," I said. "He gave me a present."

"What did he give you?"

"I can't tell you."

"Oh, come on!"

"I promised I wouldn't tell."

"I'll be your best friend."

"Well, okay. I'll show you at lunch."

During lunch, I sat at a table with my new best friend Ryan, Michael, smarty-pants Andrea, and Emily, who cries all the time even if she isn't hurt or anything. You should have seen their eyes bug out when I showed them the candy bar.

"Where did you get *that*?" Michael asked. "Your mom usually gives you carrot sticks for dessert."

"Mr. Klutz gave it to me," I explained.

"He's got a whole drawer filled with them."

"Why did he give you a candy bar?" asked Emily. I could tell she was jealous.

"Because I didn't bring in my current event," I explained.

"Wait a minute!" Andrea said, all angry and all. "You got sent to the principal's office for being bad, and instead of punishing you, he gave you a candy bar? That's not fair! I brought in *three* current events and I didn't get a candy bar."

"Maybe you should try not being so perfect all the time," I said. "You can have my carrot sticks, Andrea."

I love getting Andrea mad. She thinks

she knows everything. Whenever we have a homework assignment, she does extra work just to show Miss Daisy how smart she is and to make the rest of us look bad.

"Mr. Klutz told me he's my pal," I said, biting off a big piece of the chocolate bar right in front of Andrea's face. "He said I could come in for a candy bar any time I want one."

That last part wasn't exactly true, but it was fun to say anyway.

"The principal should give candy to students who complete their assignments," Andrea said. "Not to kids who don't."

"Yeah," Emily sniffed. She looked like

she might run out of the room crying like she usually does for no reason.

"I want to go to the principal's office!" my best friend Ryan announced.

"Me too!" Michael agreed. "I want a candy bar!"

They all watched while I finished off the candy. I licked the extra chocolate off my fingers and rubbed my tummy, just to make sure they would know how good it was.

My Big Mouth

It just so happens that I know of the perfect way to get sent to the principal's office. All you have to do is put a tack on the teacher's chair. My friend Billy told me he did this once and he got sent to the principal's office.

I waited until recess, when Andrea and

Emily ran off to play with the girls. Then I told the plan to my best friend Ryan and Michael.

"That's genius!" exclaimed my best friend Ryan.

"What if Miss Daisy gets hurt?" asked Michael.

"She won't get hurt," I told him. "She'll jump up so fast that she won't hardly feel it."

So at the end of recess, the three of us snuck back into our classroom. It was empty. Miss Daisy was eating in the teacher's room. Ryan pulled a tack out of the bulletin board and put it on Miss Daisy's chair. Then we ran out to the playground just as the end-of-recess bell was ringing. When we filed back into the class, Ryan, Michael, and I could barely look at one another because we were afraid we'd burst out laughing. I could hardly wait to see the look on Miss Daisy's face when she sat on her chair.

Well, when Miss Daisy sat down, the most amazing thing happened.

Nothing! She didn't jump up or anything. She just sat there. Me and Ryan and Michael looked at one another. How could she not feel that?

"She must have buns of steel!" Ryan whispered.

"She's like Superman."

Then I realized that I had forgotten to tell Ryan something very important. When you put a tack on the teacher's chair, you're supposed to put the tack a little bit on one side. When you put it in the middle of the chair, the tack sort of . . . well . . . you know, it doesn't have any

30

target to hit, if you know what I mean.

Miss Daisy got up to do math, not even realizing there was a tack in her butt. When she turned around to write on the chalkboard, we could see the tack was just stuck there, hanging in the middle of her backside.

Me and Ryan and Michael thought we were going to die trying to keep ourselves from laughing. It was probably the funniest thing that had ever happened in the history of the world. You should have been there!

"Excuse me," said Andrea, raising her hand to ruin everybody's fun like always. "Miss Daisy, I think there's something stuck to your skirt."

Miss Daisy turned around and pulled out the tack. "Who did this?" she demanded.

"I did!" Ryan bragged.

"Go to the principal's office, Ryan."

"All right!" Ryan whispered, pumping his fist. "I'll be back in a few minutes with a candy bar!"

"Is there anyone else who wants to go to the principal's office?" Miss Daisy asked.

"I do!" said Michael.

"Can I go again?" I said.

"Hey, I asked first!" Michael complained.

"Quiet, both of you."

Miss Daisy pretended nothing unusual had happened and went back to her lesson, but I saw her look at her chair carefully before she sat down again.

A few minutes later Ryan came back to the classroom. Mr. Klutz was with him.

"So did he give you a candy bar?" I

whispered excitedly when Ryan sat down.

"No," Ryan whispered back. "When I told him that I thought he would give me a candy bar like he gave one to you, he got really upset. He told me he was going to call my parents and have them come in to talk about what happened. I think we're all in big trouble."

Oh, man! I decided that maybe it wouldn't be such a good idea to be best friends with Ryan anymore. I should have kept my big mouth shut about the candy bar.

The Chocolate Party

When I thought about it, putting a tack on Miss Daisy's chair was a pretty dumb thing to do.

Mr. Klutz went to the front of the class. I was sure he was going to bring all of us to the torture chamber in the basement. But he didn't look all that mad, considering what we had done.

"It has come to my attention that some of the students at our school need a little extra incentive to behave and work their hardest," Mr. Klutz said. "Do you know what the word *incentive* means?"

"An incentive is a reward that encourages a person to work harder to achieve something," Andrea announced, all proud of herself. She thinks she knows everything. I hate her.

"Very good, Andrea," said Mr. Klutz. "What sort of incentive might bring out the best work in the students of our school?"

"You could give us each a million dollars," suggested Michael.

"You could make summer vacation last all year long," I said.

"How about getting rid of homework?" asked Ryan.

Miss Daisy went to the front of the

room. "Mr. Klutz can't do those things," she said. "But remember when all the students in our school read a million pages in books, and as a reward we turned the gym into a video-game arcade? That was quite successful. Mr. Klutz even dressed up in a gorilla suit for the evening, if I recall."

"How about a chocolate party?" suggested Andrea.

"Yeah!" everybody yelled.

"Mmmm," said Miss Daisy. "I like that idea!"

We all got very excited, because if there is one thing that just about everybody loves, it's chocolate. Kids started shouting out things we could have at the party, like chocolate cupcakes and chocolate fudge and chocolate bunnies and chocolate ice cream and on and on and on.

"But wait a minute," Mr. Klutz said. "What are you going to do to earn this chocolate party?"

"We could read another million pages," suggested Ryan.

"We did that already," Emily said.

"How about a million math problems?" I said.

"What a wonderful idea!" Miss Daisy beamed. Ever since we taught her how to add and subtract, Miss Daisy loved math.

"Math is hard," Ryan said. "How about a hundred math problems?"

"One million math problems," Mr. Klutz insisted. "That's my final offer. Take it or leave it."

"We'll take it!" we all yelled.

"Agreed. If the kids in our school do one million math problems, I'll throw a party with so much chocolate, you'll be sick for a week."

"I'll bring the bonbons," Miss Daisy volunteered.

"Hooray!" we all yelled, except for Ryan who looked all mad.

"I'm not going to spend my free time doing math," Ryan said. "I hate math. I wouldn't do extra math if you kissed a pig on the lips."

"Okay, as an added incentive," Mr.

Klutz said, "on the night of the party, I will kiss a pig on the lips. Have a nice day."

"All right!"

What a cool, wacky guy Mr. Klutz is! He is the coolest principal in the history of the world.

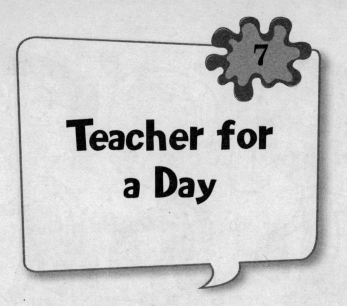

Teacher for a Day

The news about the big chocolate party blew through the school like a hurricane. Even kids who were allergic to chocolate wanted to go, just so they could see Mr. Klutz kiss a pig on the lips.

"Where is he going to get a pig?" Ryan asked during lunch the next day.

"He could try A.J.'s house," Andrea said.

"That's so funny I forgot to laugh," I said.

"I'm not entirely sure that pigs have lips," said Emily.

"Of course they have lips," I insisted. "If they didn't have lips, how could they whistle?"

"You know," Ryan pointed out, "Mr. Klutz is just trying to trick us into doing lots of math problems. That's why we're having a chocolate party."

"Who cares?" Michael said. "As long as we get the chocolate."

"I think that only students who do math problems should be allowed to come to the chocolate party," said Andrea.

"Could you possibly be any more boring?" I asked her.

As it turned out, everybody was doing math problems. The whole school started doing math problems like crazy. Even Ryan. You would have thought that Mr. Klutz was giving us gold and diamonds instead of chocolate.

"I did math problems for twenty minutes last night," Ryan bragged while we were waiting for Miss Daisy after recess.

"Oh, yeah?" Michael said. "Well, I did math problems for forty minutes last night.

Forty is twice as many as twenty. See? I just did another math problem right there!"

"Well I did math problems for an hour last night," I said. "That's fifty whole minutes."

"An hour is sixty minutes, dumbhead," Andrea told me.

I was going to tell her that *Sixty Minutes* was a TV show my parents watch, but Mr. Klutz suddenly burst into our classroom. He told us that Miss Daisy had a dentist appointment and we would have a substitute teacher for the rest of the afternoon . . . Mr. Klutz!

We all gasped.

"You're not a teacher!" I told him.

"I used to be a teacher," he said. "I taught for many years before I became a principal."

"What did you teach?" Ryan asked.

"Physics," he said.

"What's that?" I asked.

"Is that like phys ed?" asked Michael.

"Mr. Klutz, do you know that this is second grade?" Andrea pointed out. "Physics is something high school students study."

"Poppycock!" said Mr. Klutz. "You're never too young to learn something new. You may find you're smarter than you think."

"Well, if you say so."

"Physics is the study of motion and energy and force," he said. "For example, if I take a blackboard eraser in one hand and a book in the other hand, and I drop them at the same time, which one will hit the floor first?"

"The eraser!" I said. "It's smaller and lighter, so it will fall faster. Just like small, light kids run faster than big, heavy kids."

"No, the book will hit the floor first!" insisted Ryan. "Bigger and heavier things build up more speed than little things."

"I think they'll both hit the floor at the same time," said Andrea.

"Let's do a test," said Mr. Klutz.

He put the eraser in his left hand and a

paperback book in his right hand. Then he climbed on top of Miss Daisy's desk and held both objects up in the air. Then he dropped them.

The eraser and the book hit the ground at the exact same moment.

"I told you so," said Andrea. I think I hate her more every day.

"According to the laws of physics, all objects fall at the exact same rate," Mr. Klutz told us. "See? You're learning physics in second grade!"

"Wait a minute!" said Michael. "That's not a fair test because the eraser and the book are almost the same size and weight."

"Yeah," Ryan said. "Try it with different objects."

"Okay," Mr. Klutz said as he picked up a pencil off Miss Daisy's desk. Then he went over to the windowsill, where Miss

Daisy kept her collection of stuffed animals. He picked up a giraffe that was almost as big as I am. "Would this be a fair test?" he asked.

"Yeah!" we all shouted.

"Now, which object do you think will hit the floor first?" he said as he climbed up on top of Miss Daisy's desk again.

"The pencil!" some of us shouted.

"The giraffe!" other kids yelled.

"I think they will both hit the floor at the same instant," said Andrea.

"Okay, let's do a test," said Mr. Klutz.

As he raised both his arms in the air, Mr. Klutz put his foot on a crayon that was sitting on Miss Daisy's desk. It rolled a little. His foot slipped. He wobbled for a moment, trying to keep his balance. Then he pitched headfirst off the desk.

"Watch out!"

Crash!

When he hit the floor, the pencil and the giraffe went flying, and Mr. Klutz's arms and legs went in different directions. It was just about the funniest thing that ever happened in the history of the world. You should have been there.

We all ran over to see if Mr. Klutz was okay. He was holding his leg and moaning.

"See?" Andrea said. "All *three* objects hit the ground at the same time. The pencil, the giraffe, and Mr. Klutz. So I was right."

I hate her.

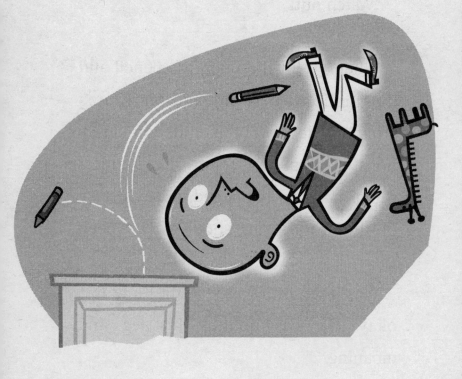

Mr. Klutz
Puckers Up

When Mr. Klutz got back from the hospital, we were all relieved to hear that he hadn't broken any bones. He was limping, though, and told us he would have to use a cane for a week.

We were afraid he might call off the chocolate party, but he was more excited about it than ever.

Everybody in the whole school got involved doing math problems so we could win the party, even the teachers.

During library period, Mrs. Roopy asked us questions like, "If the library had a hundred books and you checked out fifty of them, how many would be left in the library?"

During music period, Mr. Hynde asked us questions like, "If the school only has ten trumpets and six kids sign up to take trumpet lessons, how many more kids can sign up for trumpet lessons?"

Miss Daisy made a big tote board so we would know how many math problems we had completed. Every day, she tallied up all the math problems on her tote board.

It wasn't long before the school had finished a million math problems.

Andrea did the problem that put us

over the top—of course. I hate her.

On the night of the chocolate party, you should have seen the gym! They had music and games, and tables were set up with chocolate chip cookies, chocolate cake, chocolate muffins, and even broccoli covered with chocolate. Yuck!

By the end of the party, I thought I was going to throw up. It was the greatest night of my life.

At nine o'clock somebody came in with this big pig on a leash. I don't know where they got it. The zoo, I guess. We all watched as the pig was brought over to Mr. Klutz. He wrinkled his face up and acted like he was all disgusted

(Mr. Klutz, that is, not the pig).

When he bent over and kissed the pig
on the lips, the whole school went crazy.

Even the pig freaked out, oinking and squealing and running around the gym until the grown-ups were able to catch it.

It was a real Kodak moment, if you ask me.

I Pledge Allegiance to Mr. Klutz

"I want to congratulate all you kids," Mr. Klutz said over the loudspeaker on Monday morning during announcements. "You did it! One million math problems. That's quite an accomplishment! See, all you needed was a little incentive.

"This has been such a huge success that

I have decided to challenge you again," he continued. "Election Day is coming up in November. This is a very important day in America. I think every child in this school should write an essay about what it means to have elections. And if you achieve this goal by Election Day, I will climb the flagpole in front of the school and recite the Pledge of Allegience when I get to the top."

"I hope he doesn't hurt himself again," said Emily.

"I'll write my essay during recess," said Andrea, who always does everything the second any grown-up tells her to instead of waiting as long as possible, like a normal kid.

"Couldn't we just write one essay for the whole class?" I asked Miss Daisy. "That would be a lot easier."

Mr. Klutz's voice came out of the loud-speaker again. "I know some of you will ask if you can write a class essay. The answer is no. If you want to see me shinny up the flagpole, each student must write their own essay. That's my final offer. Take it or leave it. And I'll tell you what. When we have all the essays, I will send them to the president to read. Have a nice day."

The thought of the president of the United States reading our personal words was pretty cool, I had to admit. Everybody finished their Election Day essays so quickly, we were done a week before Election Day. Some kids (like Andrea) even wrote two essays.

On the morning of Election Day, all the students and teachers gathered on the grass in front of the school. Mr. Klutz came out of the door. He was wearing a red, white, and blue Uncle Sam costume. He also had on sneakers and one of those harnesses that lumberjacks use to climb trees. His leg was all better and he didn't walk with a cane anymore.

We all let out a roar when Mr. Klutz started to shinny up the flagpole. I was a little afraid that he was going to fall and break his leg or something, but he didn't. For a principal, he was a good climber!

When he got to the top, we all recited the Pledge of Allegience with him. Then everybody let out a cheer.

When he was sliding down the flag-pole, Mr. Klutz got his foot caught in the rope that holds the flag. As he was trying to get his foot loose, his hand slipped and he fell. The next thing we knew, Mr. Klutz was hanging upside down from the flagpole. His Uncle Sam hat fell off.

Everybody gasped.

Mr. Klutz was just hanging there, halfway up the flagpole, like he was another flag or something. It would have been the funniest thing in the history of the world if we didn't honestly think Mr. Klutz was going to fall and land on his head.

"Help!" he shouted. "My foot is caught in the rope!"

"Quick! Get some pads from the gym

for him to land on!"
yelled Mrs. Roopy, the
school librarian.

"Call the fire
department!" yelled
Mrs. Cooney, the
nurse. Everybody was
running around like
crazy, and nobody
knew what to do. It
looked like Mr. Klutz
would have to just
hang there from the
flagpole all day.

"He'll figure a way
out of this," I told the

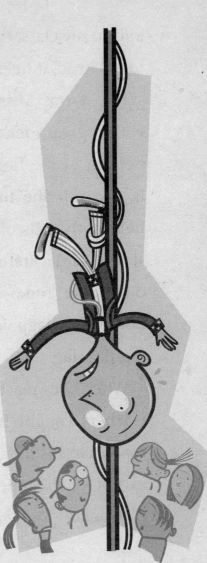

kids in my class. "When the blood rushes to his head, it helps him think."

But it was Miss Daisy who came up with a great idea. She went over to the bottom of the flagpole, where the rope is tied up. She took the knot out and held both ends of the rope tight. Then, slowly and carefully, she began to let out some rope and lower Mr. Klutz down the flagpole, just like he was a regular flag.

When he reached the bottom, the teachers caught him and loosened the rope from his foot. He was okay, he said, except for the rope burns on his leg.

"Hooray for Miss Daisy!" our class

cheered. After he was back on the ground, Mr. Klutz got up, brushed himself off, and walked up the front steps, like it was totally normal for a principal to hang upside down from a flagpole.

Mr. Klutz is nuts!

Mr. Klutz Is Getting Weirder

"Your Election Day essays were fantastic," Mr. Klutz told our class the next morning. He had a big bandage wrapped around his head. I'm guessing he must have either crashed his skateboard again or found another flagpole to fall off.

"Thank you!" we all said.

"But I was a little surprised by the number of spelling errors I found in them," he continued. "We need to improve the spelling at our school. So here is what I have decided to do. If you students can write out a list of one hundred thousand spelling words by Thanksgiving, I will dress up in a turkey costume and ride a pogo stick down Main Street."

"Yayyyyyyy!" everybody hollered.

"How about one thousand spelling words?" shouted Ryan.

"One hundred thousand spelling words," Mr. Klutz repeated. "That's my final offer. Take it or leave it. And every word must be spelled correctly. Have a nice day."

During lunch, I was sure that Andrea was going to start her list of spelling words just to show how smart she was. But she didn't. She just kind of sat there, picking at her food quietly.

"You know, I've been thinking," she finally said. "I'm beginning to wonder if something might be wrong with Mr. Klutz."

"Like what?" Emily asked.

"Maybe he has some kind of a personal problem."

"What do you mean?" Michael asked. "Mr. Klutz is a cool guy. Would you rather have a boring principal?"

"My mother is a psychologist," Andrea said, "and she says that people sometimes do weird things for reasons that are buried deep within their mind."

"What does that mean?" I asked.

"It means she thinks Mr. Klutz is nuts," said Michael.

"I didn't say that," Andrea went on. "All I'm saying is that maybe he didn't want to climb up the flagpole. Maybe he doesn't want to put on a turkey costume. Maybe he just wants people to like him, and the only way he knows to show that is to do nutty things. Maybe he's a sad, unhappy man. Maybe all he wants is a hug or something."

"That's the saddest story I ever heard!" Emily said. Then she started sobbing.

Me, Ryan, and Michael looked at one another. We all rolled our eyes up in our heads.

"Mr. Klutz is cool," Ryan said. "You're the one who has some kind of a personal problem, Andrea."

"Maybe Mr. Klutz is nuts," I said. "In fact, maybe he's not a principal at all. Did you ever think of that? Maybe Mr. Klutz escaped from a home for the criminally insane and he's just pretending to be a principal. Maybe our real principal is tied up to a chair in the dungeon down in the basement. My friend Billy told me—"

"There is no dungeon down in the basement," Emily insisted. "That's just one of those urban legends."

"Sure, that's just what he wants us to believe!" I told Emily. "He doesn't want us to know our real principal is tied up to a chair down there. He probably tortures him during summer vacation."

"I think you guys are nuts," Emily said.

"I'm worried about Mr. Klutz," Andrea said, biting her fingernails.

The Last Straw

I don't know if all that mumbo jumbo Andrea said was true or not. But I had to admit, Mr. Klutz was acting weirder and weirder.

After we finished the list of a hundred thousand spelling words and he pogo sticked down Main Street in a turkey costume, he offered to paint his bald head orange if our school got the highest reading score in the county. We did, and he came into school the next day with an orange head.

Then he offered to let every kid in the school shoot a Ping-Pong ball at him if

we collected enough box tops to buy new computers for the school media center. We did that, too.

It was fun shooting Ping-Pong balls at Mr. Klutz, but even I was beginning to worry that there was something troubling him.

And then came the day when it was obvious to everybody that Mr. Klutz had gone off the deep end. It was at the end of morning announcements. Miss Daisy had stepped out of the room for a minute.

"Boys and girls," Mr. Klutz said over the loudspeaker, "winter vacation is coming up. If the students at our school read with their parents for one million minutes before school lets out, I will bungee-jump off the roof of the school dressed as Santa Claus!"

Me and Ryan and Emily and Andrea and Michael all looked at one another.

"That's the last straw!" Andrea said.

"There are plenty of straws," I told her. "Do you want me to get you one?"

"She means we can't take this anymore," Ryan told me.

"Is that what the last straw means?" I asked. "I always wondered what the last straw meant."

"At first I thought Mr. Klutz was just a funny guy," Andrea said seriously. "And he is. But he's also a deeply disturbed man. We've got to do something. If he keeps going like this, he might hurt himself again. Or even worse. If we don't stop him and something terrible happens, it would be our fault."

"I never thought of it that way," I said.

"What can we do?" Emily asked. "We're just kids."

"We have to have an intervention," Andrea said.

"What's that?" Ryan asked.

"It's when you sit down and tell somebody they have a problem," Andrea explained. "You force them to do something about it. My mother has to do interventions all the time."

"I'm not telling Mr. Klutz he has a problem," Ryan said.

"Me neither," agreed Michael.

"A.J., you started this whole thing," Andrea told me.

"I did not!"

"Sure you did. You were the one who gave him the idea to give out incentives for learning in the first place."

"That's true," the others agreed, looking at me like I was a criminal or something.

"All I did was hit a puck into Annette," I said.

"A.J., you've got to tell Mr. Klutz that if he bungee-jumps off the roof, we're not going to read one minute with our parents," Andrea said. "Two can play at this game. If he's going to do crazy things, we won't read any more books. We won't spell any more words. We won't do any more math problems. We won't learn anything."

I couldn't believe I was hearing this from Andrea. Her idea of having fun is to read the dictionary during recess. If she was willing to give up learning, she must be really serious about Mr. Klutz and his problems.

"But if we stop learning stuff," I protested, "we'll get dumber."

"In your case," Andrea told me, "that would be impossible."

A Hard Bargain

That afternoon we talked Miss Daisy into letting us go to Mr. Klutz's office for a meeting.

"We need to speak with Mr. Klutz," Andrea told the school secretary. "It's very important."

"It's a matter of life and death," Ryan said.

The secretary let us in. Mr. Klutz wasn't hanging from the ceiling or anything. He had on boxing gloves and he was punching his punching bag.

"May I help you kids?" he asked.

"Go ahead, A.J.," Andrea said, giving me a shove from behind.

"Mr. Klutz," I told him, "we have come to make a deal with you."

"Really? What kind of deal?"

"We decided that we will read a million minutes with our parents, but only if you don't jump off the roof."

"Only if I *don't* jump off the roof?" he

said, looking puzzled. "But I was going to jump off the roof as an incentive to encourage you to read with your parents at night."

"Well, we're going to read with our parents at night as an incentive to make you *not* jump off the roof."

"This is highly unusual," Mr. Klutz said. "I thought the principal should offer the students incentives, not the other way around."

"Your incentives have been getting more and more dangerous," Andrea told him. "We're afraid that you might get killed trying to help us learn."

"Yeah, and if you die, we'll feel guilty," I added.

"Now, let me get this straight," Mr. Klutz said. "I offered to jump off the roof if you read a million minutes at night with your parents. But you are saying you will only read a million minutes with your parents if I don't jump off the roof. Correct?"

"That's right," we said.

"What if I jumped off the basketball backboard in the gym into a swimming pool filled with foam blocks?" Mr. Klutz asked. "Would that be okay?"

"No!" we all said.

"Can I wear a suit made of bubble wrap and jump off the stage in the auditorium?"

"No!"

"No jumping off *anything*," Andrea insisted. "Not if you want us to read or write or do math. That's our final offer. Take it or leave it."

"You drive a hard bargain." Mr. Klutz sighed. "Okay, I won't jump."

"Have a nice day!" we all said.

Poor Mr. Klutz

The kids in the other grades were disappointed when they heard that Mr. Klutz had changed his mind about bungee-jumping off the roof of the school. Some of them were even mad at us for stopping him.

But when it was announced that there

would be a field trip to Water World if we reached our goal instead, they stopped being mad. Water World is probably the coolest water park in California.

A few days before vacation, the school

still hadn't reached our goal of a million minutes of reading with our parents. It looked like we were not going to make it in time.

Then Mr. Klutz got on the loudspeaker during morning announcements. "Students, there are three more nights to go before vacation," he told us. "I hate to do this, but if you don't reach your goal by Friday, the field trip to Water World will be called off and I will have no choice but to jump off the roof. Have a nice day."

After hearing that, everybody started reading with their parents like crazy. Even the sixth graders, who say that reading isn't cool. Everybody wanted to go to Water World. We reached a million minutes the day before school let out for vacation.

The field trip to Water World was awesome! They had about a hundred giant water slides, and in some of them you slid in the dark with laser beams shooting all over the place. We got to eat as much pizza and ice cream as we wanted.

They also had one of those giant, inflatable moon bounce thingies where you jump around like crazy inside it. After water sliding, eating all that junk food, and bouncing in the moon bounce, I thought I was going to throw up. It was the greatest day of my life.

Me and Ryan and Emily and Andrea and Michael went looking for Mr. Klutz to thank him. We found him standing next to the moon bounce thingy.

"Great party!" I told Mr. Klutz, and we all gave him a big hug. "If you ask me, you're the greatest principal in the history of the world."

"Thanks, A.J.!"

"See, you didn't need to bungee-jump off the school to make us learn," Andrea said.

"I guess not," Mr. Klutz said. He was looking up at the moon bounce. "But I was just thinking, if we brought one of these moon bounce things out to the front of the school, and I went up on the roof—"

"No!" we all yelled.

"I wouldn't even need a bungee cord—"

"No!"

"It's pretty soft—"

"No!"

I think it's going to be very hard work helping Mr. Klutz get over this need he has to do nutty things. Maybe by June, if the whole school works together, we might be able to cure him.

But it won't be easy.

Just how crazy is Miss Daisy?

My Weird School #1

Something weird is going on!

A.J. is a second grader who can't stand school—and can't believe his teacher hates it too!

Miss Daisy, who teaches second grade, doesn't know how to add or subtract. Not only that, she doesn't know how to read or write either. She is the dumbest teacher in the history of the world!

Don't miss *My Weird School #3:*
Mrs. Roopy Is Loopy!